JIM HENSON PRESENTS

The PHANTOM of the Muppet Theater™

by Ellen Weiss

illustrated by Manhar Chauhan

◆

Muppet Press

Produced by Blaze Int'l Productions, Inc. Printed in Hong Kong h g f e d c b a

ISBN 0-8317-6151-2

This edition published in 1991 by SMITHMARK Publishers Inc., 112 Madison Avenue, New York, NY 10016.

SMITHMARK books are available for bulk purchase for sales promotion and premium use. For details, write or telephone the Manager of Special Sales, SMITHMARK Publishers Inc., 112 Madison Avenue, New York, NY 10016. (212) 532-6600.

It was the night before the big new show at the Muppet Theater, and there was still lots to do.

Fozzie's tie needed washing, Piggy's dress had to be hemmed, and Gonzo had not finished rehearsing his spoon-juggling-while-being-shot-out-of-a-cannon act.

Piggy leaned over the balcony outside her dressing room and called down to Kermit. "Oh, Kermie," she said, "could you please help moi? I need a few people to move my wardrobe out of the way. I think Foo-Foo is somewhere back there."

A small yapping noise came from behind the wardrobe.

"In a few minutes," called Kermit. "I'm really busy now."

Piggy sighed as she looked over the balcony. "Don't worry, Foo-Foo," she called to her little dog. "Someone will save you—"

Just then, Piggy heard a heavy scraping sound from her room. Her wardrobe was being moved! Out popped Foo-Foo, yipping loudly. He raced out the door and hopped into Piggy's arms.

"Thank you!" Piggy said brightly, peering into her dressing room to see who had come to her aid. But there was no one there.

Piggy felt a strange little chill.

Outside, in front of the theater, Scooter was raking leaves off the path. He stopped to rest for a moment and put his hands into his pockets to warm them.

What was this? There was a note in his left pocket.

Scooter, someone had written, *please check the leak in the roof. Look for it right above center stage.*

"That Kermit," Scooter chuckled to himself as he climbed the long, winding stairs to the roof. "With all the things he has to do today, he still never stops thinking about the theater."

Scooter opened the door to the roof and climbed outside. He made his way slowly to the area over the middle of the stage, and sure enough, there was a nice-size hole.

Scooter hammered down some new shingles. "There," he said. "Now nobody will get wet during the show."

It was a beautiful night, lit by a million stars. Scooter sat down on the roof for a few minutes. He was happy to be there. He loved working for Kermit at the Muppet Theater.

Then, Scooter got up to go downstairs. As he did, a little breeze tickled him on the back of his neck, and he thought he heard a noise.

"Kermit?" he said uncertainly, looking at the trapdoor. "Is that you?" But Scooter was alone . . . at least as far as he could tell.

Meanwhile, downstairs, Gonzo was rooting around in a large barrel full of props. "Janice?" he called, because he had seen her nearby. "Will you do me a favor and hand me a flashlight? I can't see a thing in here."

A flashlight was put into his hand. "Thanks," he said to Janice, not removing his head from the barrel. "I'm looking for that big plastic ball of fungus, and—oh, here it is!"

Gonzo straightened up, holding his fungus, but when he turned to give the flashlight back to Janice, she was nowhere in sight.

"That's funny," he murmured.

As he headed back to his dressing room, he felt a chilly wind wrap itself around him. "Window must be open," he muttered to himself, looking up.

But the window was closed.

A little later, down in the basement, Fozzie was looking for a box of light bulbs. *Gosh*, he thought to himself, *I hate to come down here. It's dusty, and it's dark, and—*

Aaagh! Suddenly, Fozzie fell down the Big Hole! Everybody knew about the Big Hole in the corner of the basement, but everybody always forgot about it, and that's just what Fozzie had done. Now he was wedged in up to his waist.

"Help!" he moaned. "Oh, help!" But he knew nobody would be able to hear him.

All of a sudden, Fozzie felt a pair of strong arms circle around him under his arms, grab him tightly, and pull him out of the Big Hole.

Fozzie, shaken but relieved, peered into the darkness. "Animal?" he guessed. "Is that you?" Animal was the only one strong enough to pull him out like that.

But nobody answered.

Upstairs, the band was setting up. It was time for the final dress rehearsal. "Okay," announced Kermit. "Everybody on stage!"

One by one, the cast straggled in.

First, Piggy appeared. "Thanks for getting my wardrobe moved before," she said to Kermit. "I know you were busy."

"Gee, Piggy," said Kermit. "What are you talking about? I never got around to it."

"Well, then, who did?" asked Piggy. She was starting to feel very strange.

Then, Scooter came in.

"Hi, Kermit," he said cheerfully. "Thanks for putting that note about the roof into my pocket. The leak's all fixed now."

"Scooter, I never put a note into your pocket," said Kermit.

"Well—er—then, who did?" asked Scooter.

Gonzo was peering into his cannon when Janice came in. "Hey, Janice," he called over to her. "Thanks for handing me that flashlight before. I tried to thank you, but you were gone."

"That's really nice of you, Gonzo," said Janice. "But I've been rehearsing with the band downstairs. Are you okay?"

"I *was* okay," said Gonzo. "Now I'm not so sure."

The trapdoor from the basement opened up in the middle of the stage. Up popped Fozzie, looking dirty and confused. He shook his head to clear it.

"Oh, Animal, there you are," he said. "Was that you who pulled me out of the Big Hole?"

"Big Hole?" echoed Animal. "Me? No!"

"Gosh," said Fozzie. "Then who did?"

Everybody looked at each other.

"Uh, gang?" said Kermit. "Do you get the feeling there's something strange going on around here?"

"I'm not sure," said Scooter. "But I have a feeling we might not be alone, Kermit."

"What do you mean?" said Piggy, shivering slightly.

There were two cackles from the box at the side of the theater. Statler and Waldorf were sitting in their usual seats, waiting for something to go wrong.

"The theater is haunted!" laughed Waldorf. "I always knew no live audience would stand for the stuff you put on!"

"I'll bet your audience will be full of ghosts tomorrow night," snickered Statler.

"That's right. They'll all be yelling *boooo!*" Waldorf chimed in with glee.

"Well, gang," said Kermit, ignoring Statler and Waldorf. "Ghosts or no ghosts, we have to get back to work. There's nothing more important than putting on a good show."

"That's right," everybody agreed.

And so they worked for the rest of that evening and through the next day, hammering, sawing, sewing, rehearsing, and running around. They didn't even have time to think about whether or not there was a ghost.

At last, it was show time. The audience was packed with excited people.

The lights dimmed, and the curtain went up—a little crooked, a little squeaky, but it worked.

There was music from the band, there was dancing and singing, there were funny jokes, and the show rolled along just fine. The audience was loving it.

Finally, they got to the part near the end when the lights
would go out, and then, for the grand finale, Gonzo would be
shot from his cannon.

Down went the lights.

Booom! went Gonzo's cannon.

"Help!" yelled Gonzo. "I'm stuck!"

The audience laughed and clapped. They thought it was part of the show. But the other performers knew it wasn't. There was Gonzo, dangling by one foot from the ropes high overhead. He was in real danger!

Kermit thought fast. "Take a bow, everyone!" he whispered. "Quickly!"

They all bowed. The audience thought the show was over. They clapped and clapped, and Scooter hurriedly closed the curtain.

"Now," Kermit said as soon as the curtain was closed, "we've got to get Gonzo down . . . in a hurry!"

"I could try climbing up there," said Scooter.

"It's too dangerous," said Kermit. "Those ropes are old and moldy. I don't know if they'd hold two people."

"Gonzo jump! Animal catch!" bellowed Animal.
"No, Animal," said Kermit. "You might miss. Besides, he's all tangled up."

As they stared up at Gonzo, who was turning a bit bluer than usual, Kermit suddenly noticed a shadowy something in the ropes above.

"Look!" he said to the others. "Am I seeing things, or is that somebody up there?"

"It *is* somebody!" Piggy gasped. "But what is he *doing* up there?"

The man slowly made his way over to Gonzo. Then he began to untangle Gonzo's foot from the ropes. "Put your arms around me," he said.

Gonzo clung to the man for dear life, and—*whoosh!* They swung down and landed safely right in the middle of the stage.

"Nice costume," said Gonzo to his rescuer when they were both on their feet again. "Although it's a little dusty—*ah-choo!*"

"Thank you for saving Gonzo," Kermit added. "But . . . who *are* you?" Kermit stared at the man. Somehow, he looked familiar.

"My name is John Stone," said the man.

"That's strange," Piggy said. "The name of the man who built this theater was John Stone."

"At your service, lovely lady," said John Stone, bowing low.

"That's it!" Kermit suddenly gasped. "I know why you look so familiar! There's a portrait of John Stone in my office... and you're exactly like him!"

"But John Stone built this theater in eighteen-oh-two!" Piggy gasped.

"Correct," said the man. "I suppose you could call me—"

"A *ghost!*" everyone said together.

"I'm afraid that's true," John Stone sighed. "I have been haunting this theater for nigh on two hundred years now. But I do not usually interfere . . . unless I see that I am needed."

"Mr. Stone," Piggy asked, "why have you stayed in this theater for all these years?"

"I just could not leave," John Stone replied. "I was an actor in my day, and this theater means a great deal to me. Why, I played Hamlet on this very stage. Besides," he added, "you put on such a wonderful show."

"Thanks," said Kermit.

"You wouldn't mind my staying here for another hundred years or so, would you?" John Stone asked.

"Oh, no!" everyone said together. "Not at all!"

"Thank you," John Stone said. "And if you ever need me . . . especially you, lovely lady," he added, turning to Piggy, "just call. I'll be nearby."

And with that, John Stone ever so slowly. . . disappeared.

"Oh, wow," said Janice.

"Did I really see what I think I saw?" said Fozzie.

"Hmmm," said Kermit.

The clock struck twelve. One by one, the Muppets drifted over to the door, each lost in his or her own thoughts.

Kermit was the last to leave. As he turned the key in the lock, he paused. "Good night, Mr. Stone," he whispered.

And he thought he felt the lightest little breeze on his cheek.